The Wayne
Manifesto

David
McRobbie

Illustrated by
Steve
Axelsen

2

I am sick of conforming to the demands of parents, sister, aunties, uncles, teachers, and a certain fat animal of the cat variety who expects me to open doors and windows to let him in or out when there is a cat door through which he can come and go very easily.

But does Fat Cat come in his little door? No, not him!

That is only one of the things that makes me sick. A lot of other events do not meet with my approval. For example, I am sick of being the youngest in the family and this being used as an excuse whenever anyone wants anything nimble done, like getting up and turning down the volume on the television or answering the telephone.

SCREECH

"Change to Channel 2, Wayne," Dad says weakly as he slumps in his comfortable chair. "Your legs are younger than mine."

Haw! What baloney! Of course they are! If I had the money, I'd buy him a leg transplant so he'd never be able to say that again!

47 The Daily Global Investigator

Plumber receives new set of legs in transplant

By NIK LIZARDSON and AAP

AUSTRALIA, Friday: 'It feels good to have young legs again', said grateful plumber, William Wilson after receiving the legs of a glamorous New York fashion model in the world's first controversial double limb transplant.

'My mates all take the mickey', said Mr Wilson. 'They keep asking me to hitch up the leg of my overalls and show them a bit of leg. I'm looking forward to trying out some of those stockings with little flowers up the side.

*T*he *Wayne Manifesto* is an idea I got when my friend Squocka Berrington wrote away to Russia and asked for some pictures of people doing a clog dance. Instead, they sent him *The Communist Manifesto* by K. Marx, who is the brother of Chicko, Harpo, Gummo, Groucho and Sloucho (the slovenly one).

There weren't any pictures in *The Communist Manifesto,* so Squocka gave it to me and I read it but couldn't get past the first sentence because it contained more big words than my feeble brain could handle. My teacher Mr. Dellafield sprang, nay, leaped to the rescue and explained it was a public declaration that helped guide the destiny of the Russian people.

He said it was a statement saying what things had been like in the past and letting everyone know what was going to happen in the future. It was just what I needed, so I wrote out a manifesto for myself so eveyone could marvel at my grasp of politics and stuff:

THE WAYNE MANIFESTO

1. I will enjoy showers for as long as I LIKE.
2. I will NOT collect the morning paper when newsboy Ronnie Teeth hurls it under the big spreading bush in the front garden.
3. My room will look like a rubbish dump until I am Good and Ready to tidy it up.
4. I will NOT get up and answer the telephone every single time when it rings during family television viewing.
5. I will play my cassettes LOUDLY because that is the way they are meant to be heard.
6. I will NOT be the only one who gets up to adjust the volume or change channels on the television.

Fastened to the fridge door with a magnetic moon and a little plastic clown, my manifesto looks very impressive.

Squocka thinks Wayne Manifesto sounds like a Corsican soccer league half-back so he acts like a radio commentator or something:

"And Wayne Manifesto scoops up the ball and oh, he drops it! Good thing the game hasn't started yet or that could have been a costly error on Manifesto's part."

Mom sees my public declaration on the refrigerator door and pauses long enough to read it. I can see she is one impressed mother. She'll tell all the neighbors, that's for sure.

"Our Wayne's got a manifesto," she'll say proudly. They won't know what it is, so they'll just shake their heads and say, "What next? Tut, tut, tut," and "Young people today," and "Our Gerald's got a Suzuki."

Mom can be maddening at times because she doesn't say *anything at all* about my six points.

Next morning, I get up early to take my shower and this is day one of *The Wayne Manifesto.* Oh, it's lovely! I turn on the water and face this way and that as the hot bubbles massage my body. Luxury!

*T*hen it happens. All of a sudden, the water turns cold! Sharp icicles spear through me. Freezing hailstones pelt my chest and shafts of coldness drum on my bottom.

I spring out from under and go "Yoobba, yabba, ye!" Strange words from a long-lost language which mean "Hasn't it turned cold all of a sudden?"

I wrap my freezing person in a towel and go padding out to Mom to complain about the plumbing. I am totally soapy with goose pimples like watermelons.

"Shower's gone cold, Mom," I say through chattering teeth. It is hard to speak with an icicle dangling from your nose. "Freezing!"

"That's because I turned off the hot water supply," Mom says calmly, showing me the key to the cupboard. She drops the key into her pocket in a way that tells me she is not going to bring it out again.

"But what about my manifesto?" I say. "Point one—long showers."

Mom consults the manifesto.

"Says nothing there about *hot* showers," she says and turns away to make herself a slice of toast.

"But, but," I say. But Mom's not listening. I plead, I protest, I grovel and whine, but she ignores me.

9

"Oh, are you still here?" she says when the toast pops up. She listens to my pleas then nods wisely.

"I think we can agree on a compromise, Wayne." She takes up a pen and changes item one until it says:

I will enjoy *hot* showers for four minutes.

"All right, that's a fair compromise," I say. Mom lets me have another two minutes of hot water to wash off the frozen soap and bubbles.

Later, I hear my big sister Patricia spending *five minutes* in the shower. I know this because she sings a whole song right through then starts on another one. I bet she's got her guitar in there too!

I complain to Mom, who says Patricia is a girl and she's older than me, so there's more of her to wash. I decide to raise this question during science when we get to the part where anyone can ask any questions they like without feeling embarrassed. But in the end, I chicken out because she's my sister after all, and I do not want her to be the subject of a science lesson.

I come down for breakfast and find Dad is already there.

"Oh, Wayne, run out and get the paper for me," Dad says. Wouldn't you know it, Ronnie Teeth has struck again, and the paper is under the big spreading bush next to a dead frog, which will nauseate me if I go near it.
them.

Well, that's that then! I go back to the breakfast table without the morning paper.

"Sorry, Dad," I say. "Point two of my manifesto. I refuse to crawl in for the paper because Ronnie Teeth has done it again like he always does just to annoy me."

D ad swings around in his chair and consults the manifesto and sniffs.

"Looks like there's room for a bit of compromise, Wayne," he says and takes up a pencil and changes things around a bit. Now it reads:

I will collect the morning paper *with the long garden rake* when newsboy Ronnie Teeth hurls it under the big spreading bush in the front garden.

I try to argue, but Dad just tells me the rake is in the shed with the other garden tools, so I go out grumbling. Mom gives Dad a big smile, so that's one good thing to come out of my manifesto. More people should compromise. It brings families together and makes parents smile at each other in the morning.

Later, I hear Mom on the telephone telling Mr. Teeth, the newsagent, she is not happy with the delivery arrangements.

"Is that so, Mrs. Wilson?" Mr. Teeth says on the telephone. (I can hear this because of my super sensitive ears and the fact that I am listening on the extension.) "Well, I don't know how to improve the service, so if you don't like it you know what to do."

"Fair enough," Mom says. "I'll do just that, Mr. Teeth. Remember, you need me. I don't need you." Clunk. That's telling him. Mom folds her arms and waits by the telephone and sure enough, as soon as Mr. Teeth finds our number, it rings.

13

"Let's not be hasty, Mrs. Wilson." He is super grovelly.

"Oh, I'd never be hasty, Mr. Teeth." Mom is full of charm. She tells him about Ronnie and his feud with me, and Mr. Teeth promises the paper will be delivered on our doorstep from now on.

Even Mr. Teeth is compromising now and doing it Mom's way. To protect his identity and avoid ruining his business, I have not used the newsagent's real name. I am kind that way. I use the name "Mr. Teeth" because his whole family smiles all the time.

They spent hundreds of dollars at the dentist, so if you go into their store you need sunglasses because of the dazzling smiles they bestow on their customers. But do not go around looking for a smiling newsagent in the hope of identifying the "Teeth" family, because it may or may not be them.

*B*ack to the Manifesto and the episode of my untidy bedroom.

I go to school one day, leaving a few things scattered around on the floor and hanging from the light fixture on the ceiling, but that is only a pair of underpants which got kicked up there when I was aiming them at Fat Cat and missed.

When I come home, tired and exhausted, I find the contents of the kitchen trash can are on the floor of my room. Not only that, there is a bunch of old newspapers in a corner. Dad has left some things on my bed—an old fishing rod, a basket, and a rain boot. Patricia's old lovelorn magazines and empty makeup bottles are on my desk. It looks like they are using my room as a rubbish dump. Next thing you know, the town will be at it too!

All right, if they want to play it tough, then so can little Wayne. I ignore the rubbish and say nothing. But as the days pass, my dear family dump more and more stuff in there until I have trouble finding my bed. This is too much, so I go downstairs and inquire of my female parent what is going on with all the rubbish in my room, including the contents of the kitchen trash.

"I thought you *wanted* your room to be a rubbish dump, Wayne," Mom says, looking at my manifesto.

"But only *my* rubbish," I say. Mom takes up her pen.

"A bit more compromise, Wayne?"

A few minutes later, item three of the manifesto reads:

My room will look like a rubbish dump until I *tidy it up, which will be sooner rather than later.*

I am not sure about this one, so I argue and ask everyone to come and collect their own rubbish. I rant and rave and say how unfair it is, not to mention unhygienic. I say I'm being picked on, but Mom assures me it is a good compromise. So I start to clean up and lo, Mom comes in and helps. Then Patricia removes her stuff too, and Dad wanders in with a big garbage bag and before you know it, my room is spic and span. But nobody spots the underpants on the light fixture.

Then comes one of those moments of sheer horror, a time in a young man's life when he wishes the floor would open up and swallow him.

We are watching television and taking turns at saying "Ooh!" and "Ah, would you believe it," and "It's time we got a new one, Dad." The reason is, our television set is very old and the picture tube will go any day now—so the repair man is fond of telling us every time he comes. The telephone rings.

"Get that, Wayne," Dad says. He is trying to be engrossed in something in which I am also attempting to be engrossed.

"What about my manifesto?" I remind him. The phone rings on and on and no one moves.

"Might be for you, Wayne," Mom says. She is also engrossed.

"Might be for Patricia," I say, giving my sister a sly dig. "Your boyfriend calling on the car phone."

"Rupert's playing tennis tonight," she says, also engrossed. The phone still rings, so Mom finally gets up and answers it.

It's a triumph for me. The manifesto works. I have made a stand and declared independence.

"Hello," Mom says into the mouthpiece. "No, Wayne says he's not going to answer the telephone, so you can talk to him tomorrow."

"Looks like it's for you, Wayne," Dad murmurs.

"Who is it, Mom?" I say, starting up to take the receiver from her, but Dad restrains me.

"Let your mother handle it," he says, but whoever's on the phone has made Mom angry.

"Listen, Fish Features!" she snaps. "My boy doesn't want to answer the phone and if he doesn't want to do something, then that's all right with this family, you got that, Drain Brain?"

Drain Brain, eh? Must be an intellectual. Mom pauses. "Oh yeah, you and what army?"

"Mom!" I say in some alarm. This could be embarrassing, but Mom has her dander up and there's no holding her.

"*O*h yeah, well Wayne says go fry your eyeballs and play with the smoke!" She hangs up and storms back to her chair. "What a nerve that guy's got!"

"Quite right." Dad passes her the box of cookies.

"Bravo!" Patricia says and applauds.

"Em, who was it, Mom?" I say uneasily. (After all, it *was* for me!) "Maybe I should call back or something."

"**N**o, don't bother, son," Mom pats my hand. "Just you sit there and enjoy your television. I can handle old Dellafield any day."

Instantly, and with sharp needles under my fingernails, I die a million deaths! Hot skewers pierce my skin, and a million draggy steam irons make creases in my body!

I completely forget the television program and its flickering, non-color, rolling-over images with rotten sound. Later, we agree to more compromises. The manifesto now reads:

I will *take my turn at answering* the telephone *like everyone else in the family.*

Next day at school, I tippy-toe in the gates and try to be very small. In fact, I make myself so tiny the first grade teacher thinks I'm one of her kids and rosters me as goldfish monitor for April.

Warily, I watch old Dellafield in case he singles me out for a firing squad or something. He's the sort of man who'd insist you have a final cigarette before they shoot you, even though everyone knows smoking is a health hazard.

But Old Dellafield, or Mr. Dellafield to give him his full title, is not in a bad mood at all. In fact, he is quite nice, but I do not pluck up the courage to ask him if he telephoned me at home last night.

Me:　Sorry I wasn't there when you called last night, Roger.

Roger:　Quite all right, old chap. I spoke to your Mother instead. Charming woman.

Me.　Yes, she is rather wonderful. Did she have anything special to say, Roger?

Roger:　Oh yes, I had to chuckle at some of her witty suggestions and her vivid descriptions of me. Yes.

I begin to smell a rat. Who *was* Mom talking with last night? It wasn't old Dellafield; otherwise I'd have been strung up by the thumbs for most of the day. I decide to try the direct approach.

"Mom, who *was* on the phone last night?"

She smiles a secret smile and picks up the telephone receiver and presses her finger to hold the cradle down.

"Listen, Dellafield," she snarls into the mouthpiece. "I thought I told you to stop bugging my boy, Wayne!"

"There was nobody there!" I say with a huge surge of relief. Mom puts the telephone receiver down and smiles a sweet momly smile.

"They hung up just as I got there, so I thought I'd have a bit of fun," she says.

"Oh, Mom," is all I can say. Then she gets talking about my manifesto and I tell her I just want to do my own thing.

"Oh, I wish I could do my own thing too," she sighs. "But I've got to think of other people all the time. One day, when I'm an old and lonely Grandma with no one else around, then I'll do my own thing."

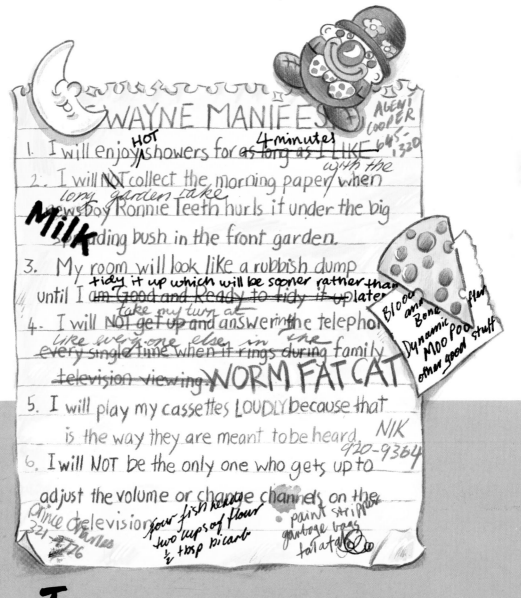

WAYNE MANIFESTO

1. I will enjoy HOT showers for as long as I LIKE 4 minutes
   ~~as long as I LIKE~~ 645-1320 AGENT COOPER
2. I will NOT collect the morning paper when with the long garden rake
   newsboy Ronnie Teeth hurls it under the big spreading bush in the front garden. Milk
3. My room will look like a rubbish dump
   until I ~~am Good and Ready to tidy it up~~ tidy it up which will be sooner rather than later
4. I will NOT ~~get up and answer~~ take my turn at the telephone ~~like everyone else in the~~
   ~~every single time when it rings during family~~
   ~~television viewing~~ WORM FAT CAT
5. I will play my cassettes LOUDLY because that
   is the way they are meant to be heard. NIK 920-9364
6. I will NOT be the only one who gets up to
   adjust the volume or change channels on the
   television Prince Charles 321-776
   four fish heads
   two cups of flour
   ½ tbsp bicarb
   paint stripper
   garbage bags
   fairatale

   Blood and Bone Dynamic flour Moo Poo other good stuff

I look at my manifesto with all the extra scribbles
on it, including a few phone numbers, bits of
shopping lists and a recipe for fish scones. I bet
K. Marx's mom didn't scribble things on his
manifesto.

"Do you think I should just tear this up then, Mom?" I say.

"Oh no, son," she says. "It's a lovely manifesto. Keep it up a little while longer—I've still got to copy out that recipe."

Dad has a different way of putting it. More direct, you might say.

We are sitting at the table having supper—just we three, Mom, Dad, and me. Patricia is out with Rupert (the nerd of the year), which is why we are calling it supper and not dinner. Mom raises the idea of me wanting to do my own thing.

"You *can't* do your own thing," Dad says. "Because you've got to come and go with people." This is a very profound thing for my father to say, so I ponder it awhile as I take the last hot dog from the plate in the center of the table.

"How do you mean, Dad?"

"You've got needs, son," he says. "You need a place for a bed, a roof overhead, food to eat, and clothes for the street."

"And the love of a good partner," Mom adds.

Dad reaches for the last hot dog and finds I've got it, so we compromise and he gets half. Well, three-quarters of it.

"You need other people to buy what you sell, son," he goes on. "Whether it's your labor, something you've made, or something you've grown. We're like a lot of little cog wheels, all spinning like clockwork, and we have to turn because our neighbors are turning. Try doing your own thing in there and you get spat out of the system. Bang! You end up bruised and whimpering with your teeth all broken."

"What your Dad means is you can only do your own thing to a certain extent and at certain times," Mom explains.

"You mean on public holidays and weekends?" I ask.

"Yes, something like that, Wayne," Dad says. "But even then there's rules and regulations so you can't go dancing on the tables."

Pondering upon my father's profound utterances, I go to my room and play a cassette very loudly. No compromise here, I declare. This is my room, my personal space, these four walls and built-in wardrobe are my territorial boundary. This floor and this ceiling and light fixture with a pair of underpants on it, they make a private world in which I can be myself and do my own thing.

Fat Cat springs up and sits on my head. When he dies, for revenge I will get him made into a set of stereo headphones.

27

*T*he door of my private space opens and in glides Patricia, filled with fun and good humor, having arrived home after an evening out.

"Wayne dear, that noise is a bit loud," she says sweetly and turns the sound down. Then with her sharp, long fingernails, she lifts the volume knob off the cassette player and drops it down her sweater.

Men have no answer to an action like that. My volume knob has found its own private space!

Patricia sweetly refuses to give it back so I have to compromise some more. Item five on the manifesto now reads:

I will play my cassettes as loudly as I can without the volume knob.

However, there is light on the horizon. Patricia says I can get my knob back only if I promise to consider the feelings of others. I do not think I want it back, knowing where it has been, but I promise anyway.

There is an air of mystery in the house. Dad and Mom are excited about something and they whisper furtively. But when I come into the room, they stop whispering and look all airy and innocent. Something is going on.

After my homework, we sit down to watch television, and I am the one who has to walk around the room holding the aerial to get the best reception. Ha! That's a laugh! Once they actually made me climb out the window and stand in the front yard while everyone sat inside saying "That's fine, keep it there, son." It was pouring rain at the time, and I was scared I'd be struck by lightning or spotted by someone important in my young life, like Vicky Hill from next door.

Anyway, without leaving the living room, I finally discover the right position for the aerial and we watch a program about new technology and television sets of the future. At the end of the evening's viewing, Dad makes a great show of groaning and grunting and looking as if it's hard to get out of his chair.

"That's it for tonight," he says. "Time to finish with the old TV." With his back all bent and his brow all furrowed, he looks so sad and elderly, that I take pity on him.

"I'll turn it off, Dad," I say.

"No, let your Dad do it," Mom says. "You just sit there, Wayne. After all, you've got your manifesto. Item six."

I'd nearly forgotten about it, and in fact, I am getting fed up with my manifesto.

Dad limps towards the television. He turns it off, pulls out the wires at the back, picks up the whole box of tricks, puts the aerial on top, and marches out with it. My eyebrows rise a millimeter. Mom just looks at the *TV Times* and pays no attention.

Out in the yard, I hear a sudden crash and a tinkle of breaking glass as something gets hurled into the back of Dad's truck. My eyebrows go up another millimeter. Dad comes in and sits down again. again.

"That's that," he says. "No more television. No more fighting and bickering, no more asking Wayne to get up to change channels. Just peace and contentment and conversation as a family.

"Well done, Bill," Mom says.

"That was a bit drastic!" I say. "I did *offer* to turn it off, Dad."

"Oh no, son," Dad says. "It wasn't your turn. Besides—you've got your manifesto."

"Yeah, but we don't have a television set anymore!" I am devastated. But this is where Mom and Dad break out in big smiles. Dad gets up and goes to the front room and rolls in a brand new, 24-inch television set on its own little wheels, and it's even got a remote control! Oh, joy of joys!

I go to my manifesto and make another compromise. Item six now reads:

Wayne shall be the one who works the remote controller.

Dad inspects what I've written.

"I think that one could do with a bit more compromise," he says. He crosses out "Wayne" and writes "Dad" instead.

Wouldn't you know it!

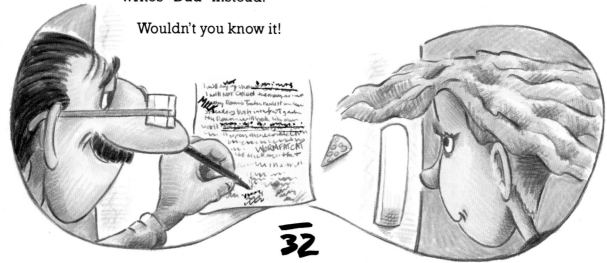